The Pet Shop Around The Corner

By Katleen Nielsen

Chapter One :

Acquiring a pet

I walked into a pet shop today, looking

for something soft and cuddly. After spending some time with the chinchilla's, hamsters, guinea pigs and squirrels, my attention got caught by a huge aquarium with dozens of tiny little mice. They looked like loads of fun, seeing as they were tumbling all over each other, nibbling each other's ears and chasing each other's tails. They uplifted me in such a way that I cheerfully turned to the shopkeeper and asked her if I could have a few for my domestic enjoyment.

The shopkeeper, however, raised a mournful eyebrow and informed me of the fact that these mice were not for sale.
When I asked her why not, she paused for a bit, then drew closer, all the while checking that we were not being overheard by some innocent bystanders .
« These are for the snakes... », she almost whispered in my ear.
« What do you mean by that ? » I innocently replied, trying to imagine a playful scene where the snakes dashed around a bit, watching the mice for their utter amusement.

The shopkeeper gave me a surprised look.
« They eat them, you see » she whispered even more inaudibly.

In shock, I stared back at her. Surely not ! These joyful little creaures, full of life and merriment, were not just a sunday snack for those big, dozing snakes at the far end of the shop ?

The shopkeeper, registering my alarm, pulled a carefully practised sad face at me. She stayed silent.

« So...I can't even have a few ? » I trailed off. Maybe I could save some of them from a cruel fate.

« Oh yes, you can. » the shopkeeper said reassuringly. « If you buy a snake. »

How absolutely terrible. I had to pause and think. Maybe I should get a snake and train it to be good friends with the mice. Or, even better, I would make it a vegetarian. Yes, that's what I would do. Excellent plan. I'd feed the snake some lettuce and give it plenty of fresh fruit for vitamins. Because, seriously, would a snake know the difference between a mouse and an apple ? Snakes don't taste their food anyway, they just swallow it whole. I think.

I was rather happy with my own ingenuity, and so, with my most comforting smile, I asked the shopkeeper to show me the snakes.

We headed off to the back of the shop. There

were three different kinds of snakes available. The first one was curled up in a bundle, completely unaware of the outside world. It had probably just been fed. It looked sleepy, grey, and utterly uninteresting.

Number two was all black, with big yellow stripes along its sides. It jerked up its head at me right away and looked at me in a ravenous fashion. It made me feel like a freshly served leg of lamb. Too hungry, this one. And definitely not a veggie.

Over to number three. Ah, that was better. Overall green, with dots of the most lively colours. A rainbow snake. I tapped on its window. It lifted its head gently and gave me an interested look. Not hungry, but curious, as if I were some kind of a soulmate. Yes, I could definitely work with this one. It would easily understand the virtues of letting a fellow creature live.

Reassured, I turned to the shopkeeper. « This one. » I pointed. « That's the one I want. »
This time, it was the shopkeeper's turn to look at me in shock.
« The Rainforest Snake ? » she said. « Are you sure ? »
My confidence crumbled a bit.

« Is this your first snake ? » she asked.

« Yes... » I trailed off, not too sure as to where this was going.

« Then it would be better if you got another one for starters. That one, for instance », she pointed to the first one. « Much less trouble, eats and sleeps, has a relatively safe bite, stays out of your way as long as you don't touch it. Perfect for beginners. » she added.

« Oh. » I said. « So, what about this Rainforest Snake ? » I asked, « It's dangerous, then ? »

« Dangerous is an understatement. », the girl said. When you least expect it, it will slowly curl around you, smothering you slowly while you feel happy and comforted like a little baby rabbit. And next thing you know, you´re gone. »

« Oh. », I said, rather disappointed.

« And perhaps it's interesting to know... », she added in a whisper, « ...that most clients return their snakes after a few months . They get bored, or don't know how to feed them properly. We always get them back. But with the Rainforest Snake ? » she closes in on my ear. « No-one returns them. » she adds. « No-one. They never come back. Interesting, isn't it ? »

I swallow hard. For a moment, neither of us says anything.

Then, I swirl around, go over to the other side

of the shop and say :
« So, how about those rabbits ? »

Chapter Two :

The Flemish Giant

So, I got a rabbit.
Forget about those mice. They're
probably not that interesting, anyway.
And a snake ? No, thanks. No cuddle value
whatsoever. I'll pass for now.

I look at my rabbit, rather proudly. It
took me just a moment to decide which one I'd
take with me. It just sat there, waiting for me.
A tiny, white, helpless and utterly cute little
critter. It was love at first sight.

I take out the leaflet with specifications

the shopkeeper had tucked inside my box. « Flemish Giant », it reads. It says the little fluffy ball I bought will reach gigantic proportions in no sooner than 6 months. Right. I did not see that coming. But hey, a big rabbit is still a rabbit. There will just be more of it to cuddle, that's all.

« Food », reads the leaflet. « Lettuce, carrots, cauliflower, broccoli, anything green. Herbs, dried flowers, leaves and grass. » Good, it's a vegetarian. This can't go wrong.

« Habitat. » I read on. « Although the Flemish Giant can be kept indoors, it will thrive better when let outdoors at regular intervals. With the help of a rabbit shed and a moveable fence, you can keep the rabbit in any part of the garden, where it will take care of your freshly-grown grass. As from now, your lawn-mower days are over. »

Oh dear. I'll need a garden for this thing. I sigh deeply. The rabbit hasn't moved in properly yet, and it's already causing trouble. But hey, let's wait a little first. It's wintertime anyway, and too cold for being outdoorsey. And by springtime, who knows, I might have won the lottery and moved to a cozy little shack with a tiny little garden. Yes, that would be nice. There'd be a beautiful fruit tree in the middle and some strawberry bushes to line it off. Do rabbits eat strawberries ? I check the leaflet again. Nope, there's no mention of it. I'll teach it to eat strawberries then. I'm sure it will love them. Everyone loves strawberries. I smile contentedly. I'm already looking forward to living there.

For now, however, the rabbit will have to settle for the cage I bought. Looking at it, I realize I might have overdone it a tat. It fills most of my dining room. So much so, that I had to move the table out to the cellar. Which is all right, really. I can just sit on a chair in the corner and eat there. Instead of the telly, I'll just watch my rabbit. Much more interesting.

I feel uplifted already. This rabbit is going to be my Best Friend. I'll watch it eat some carefully chosen carrots, while I munch away at my half frozen, half burnt TV-dinner. It'll be perfect.

The rabbit is sitting a little huddled in the corner, wondering where its Mummy went. It doesn't want to touch the pellets I bought it and is looking perplexed by the magnum-sized water bottle that hangs on the other side of the cage. It is three times bigger than the rabbit itself. Maybe I should have listened to the shopkeeper and gotten the smallest one. Oh well, I'll just hand-feed the rabbit some droplets with my eye-drop counter. That'll do for now.

Good. Now what ? Should I take the rabbit up and cuddle it a bit ? Probably. What do mummy rabbits usually do ? Maybe I'll let it suckle on my finger a little. Yes, good plan, I'll do that. Carefully, I take it out of the cage, whilst making little comforting noises as I imagine a mummy rabbit would. There. It's sitting on my lap. I stroke it for a bit and then gently insert my finger into its mouth.

Ouch ! It's got teeth ! And darn big ones for such a tiny creature. Of course, it's a rodent, isn't it ? What did I expect ?

I carefully put the bunny down on my chair while I get up to fetch a plaster from the kitchen. I'm bleeding like a pig. Five pieces of kitchen towel later I start wondering whether I should call an ambulance. Are there main arteries running through my index finger ? Could I actually bleed to death here, standing in my own kitchen ? While I'm contemplating which pyjama's I should take with me to hospital, the bleeding starts to subside. Phew. Safe again. I wrap a king-size plaster around my finger and return to my dining-room.

But hello ? Where's the rabbit ? Didn't I just put it on the chair ? Thoughtfully,I scan the room. Well, it's not in its cage. Where then ? Oh God. It's under the pile of furniture I moved to the other side of the room, isn't it ? I reluctantly look under the two cupboards, five lamps and three chairs stacked on top of each other. Nothing. Cautiously, I squat on all fours. It's really dark under there, I can't see a thing. I'll just get a broomstick, then. Maybe I can scoop it out.

I walk over to the broom closet and open it. But just as my hand reaches out for the broom, my eye catches something white and fluffy in the corner. Well, what do you know ? It's the rabbit . But... how did it get there ? The door to the closet was closed, wasn't it ? So how... ? There must be a hole somewhere. I carefully check the outside. Not as much as a peephole. This is amazing. How can this be ? Unless... my mind is racing at full speed now. Could it be... no, certainly not... and yet... it had to. Could it be... a magic rabbit ? One that can fly right through time and space into the broom closet ? But why there ? I glance around for magic objects. But of course ! What can you find in a broom closet ? A broom ! My brooms don't fly, of course, but the rabbit doesn't know that. It was probably going for the nearest thing to a cab. Thank God I found it in time, or it would have flown right back there.

So, where did this magic rabbit come from ? It had probably lived with a magician before, in a circus or something. It must have escaped somehow, and ended up in the pet shop. Maybe I should go back there and ask. But, on the other hand, it is quite tempting to keep the rabbit for myself. It might be able to do some stunning tricks I can baffle my friends with. Maybe I should get a magician's top hat for it, and a pair of white gloves . What else ? I sit and think for a while.

Suddenly, the doorbell rings. I quickly close the broom closet with the rabbit still inside. Nervously, I go and open the door. It's Suze, my nextdoor neighbour.
« Hi ! », she smiles. « Do you think I could borrow some sugar ? I'm flat out and you know how a cuppa tea tastes without... »
« Of course. », I mumble « Be right back. », hoping that Suze will stay in the doorway. But, of course, Suze being Suze, she follows me into the kitchen.
« So... », she starts, giving me a curious look, « What's up, then ? Anything I should know ? Got some new furniture or something ? » she winks. « You know you can tell me. »

And there you have it. You can't hoist a bloody rabbit cage up the stairs without half the neighbourhood knowing. And Suze is the worst of them all. I think she sits by her door all day, waiting for innocent bypassers to do the Unexpected, which ranges from glueing chewing gum to the wall to being robbed in broad daylight by two Mexicans pretending to be plumbers (yes, I've tried both). And should she miss out on anything at all during the twenty-minute grocery shopping she indulges in every day, she will sniff out everything and ring at everyone's doorbell in order to find out What Happened. So, there she was. In my kitchen. Pining for details of what had caused the racket on the stairs earlier this morning.

A little miffed, I remain silent. This is no easy game. I don't want her to know about the rabbit yet, what with it being magical and all. Plus, Suze knows I'm terrible with pets. I had to babysit her cat once and, suffice it to say, there was not much left of the poor creature after that. So, there is no way I am going to tell her about my new acquisition. No way at all.

Suze, being rather thrown by the fact that I refuse to comment, stops dead in her tracks. Then, as if the sun itself had come to shine upon a brandnew world, she lights up and says : « It's Vian, isn't it ? He's moving in !»

Again, I remain silent, this time for an altogether different reason. I'm dreading what follows next.
« I knew it ! », she proclaims. « Well done, darling, you captured him at last ! I couldn't be more proud of you ! » She hugs me with the intensity of a heavy-weight wrestling champion.
« I bet you'll be as happy as a pair of turtle doves, the two of you. A perfect match, if ever there was one ! I bet Vian is already looking out for a ring, don't you think ? You'll be married before the year is over! Congratulations, my girl, congratulations ! » She is hopping from one leg to the other now, waiting for me to give the go-ahead for a wedding planner.

In shock, I hold on to the kitchen table and sit down. I need to collect my thoughts. Why ? Because, Vian, the poor man, is, unfortunately, just a figment of my imagination. I made him up in order to fend off Suze's endless harrassment as to when I would find myself someone Nice and Reliable. You know, a shoulder to cry on, a holder of hands, a rubber of feet and the perfect candidate for breeding children.

As if. Not only do I dread the thought of an ever-lasting love life, my choice of men has always been deeply upsetting for all those around me (yes, they tend to drink and drive, burp out loud and pass out in the middle of family reunions). I seem to get it wrong every time, and both my family and friends have moved to that place which is beyond stupefaction. Why can't she get anyone proper, they ask themselves. Is it a curse ? Or is it Young Folly ? She's twenty-two now, after all, and, being a looker, can catch anyone she likes. So what is it that stops her from finding the proper one for her ?

Hence Vian. Rich heir from real estate family, he dabbles with different art projects, ranging from foreign street music to painting, both on busses and underground walls. He's quite renowned in the art community and travels the world, visiting fellow artists and looking for new input. Well in his thirties, he is childless, yet exciting and adventurous and in a few words, the Love of my Life.

Not bad, is it ? Ok, maybe he isn't the 2.4 children, Volvo and suburban house type, but I've managed to convince Suze it is just a question of time until he wants to settle down with me. Of course, she ate it raw. And although she's never seen him in the six months we've been together, she believes in him like a toddler believes in Father Christmas. As for the most cunning part of my plan, consider this : even if she ever grows suspicious and wants to meet him, Vian and I will have a Big Break-Up, which will leave me shattered for life and utterly unfit for any future romance. Brilliant, isn't it ? Yes, I'm rather proud of myself.

But let's get back to the kitchen. Suze is still dancing around as if she's won a trip to Paris. I can see she's already mentally picking out her bridesmaid's dress from the local bridal shop. She doesn't waste much time, I can tell you that.

Suddenly, however, she stops in her tracks and gives me a concerned look.
« Are you all right, dear ? » she asks, a little dumbfounded by my collapsed figure at the kitchen table.
« Of course », I smile brightly. « Never better. » I get up and hand her the cup of sugar she came for. But by the furtive glances she shoots at me, I can tell my silence is killing her.

I walk out into the hallway, secretly hoping she will not harass me with further questions. I fail to come up with a good explanation for my mid-morning racket on the stairs and I'm secretly praying she will let the subject go. To my complete surprise, she doesn't utter one more word.

Suze being Suze, however, she seems to have come up with a different strategy : instead of following me down the hallway, she decides to snoop around a bit. She pops her head around the bedroom door, probably checking for new furniture. Disappointed, she moves to the living room. Nope, nothing there either. Before I can stop her, she glances inside the dining room and … boom ! There it is ! She stops in her tracks and goes all rigid. I watch her jaw drop in slow-motion. Yes, the cage is impressive. And no, there is nothing inside it. But dear woman, get a grip.

« What is THAT ? » she bellows, and I see her crumble like a pie on a children's birthday. She stares at me in despair. Gone, the dream of an upcoming wedding. Gone, the prospect of a new, settled girlfriend with a Life and a Future.

She tries to say something, but all that comes out is a deep gurgling sound. I pause and fidget a bit, hoping that she'll snap out of it and thus avoid a stroke.
« Well, what IS it ? » she finally manages to

utter.

« A cage. », I say helpfully, with a sheepish grin.

« What FOR ? » she wants to know.

« Well, not for Vian, obviously. », I giggle nervously.

But Suze just stares at me, with an intensity that draws the blood from my face.

All right, then. Here goes nothing. Reluctantly, I confess my indulgence.

« It's for an animal I bought. », I shoot her an uncomfortable look, not sure what to expect.

« An animal ? » she shrieks. « Like what, a rhinocerus ? »

« No... » I trail off. « A...rabbit. »

« A rabbit ? In this size cage ? Are you absolutely mad ? You can keep a whole flock of them in there ! »

« Yes, I know I overdid it a bit... »

« Overdid it a bit ? I could live in there myself, it's bigger than my apartment ! Plus, », she continues with a hiss, « do you not remember how completely incompetent you are with animals ? You nearly killed Mrs. Whiskers last time ! Cats are not supposed to be washed in the laundry machine ! »

«It crept in there all by itself, I didn't see it there... », I say miserably.

« Still, that doesn't explain why you blow-dried it with my most expensive hairdryer. The

cat was a complete mess, the hairdryer smelled of burnt toast, and you blew the fuses in the whole building ! Who DOES such a thing ? »
I stare guiltily at the floor, not knowing what to say.
« And don't get me started on that fateful afternoon where you had to walk Dr. Weatherhill's pekinese. You came back with a completely different dog ! How on earth did you manange that ? » Fumes were coming out of her nostrils.

Once more, I bow my head in surrender. True, I lack the necessary skills for elementary pet-keeping, but one can live in hope, can't one ? This rabbit, I'm sure, is going to save me from my airheaded ways and teach me once and for all how to parent a living creature. It'll be my Guiding Star.

« So, where is it, then ? » Suze looks around the room, scanning for unsavory rodents.
« In my broom closet. » I admit guiltily.
« What's it doing THERE ? » she rolls her eyes at me.
« Well, it kind of... ran off... » I mutter.
Suze narrows her eyes and gives me a piercing look.
« Well, show it to me, then. » she says, not taking no for an answer.

So I sigh deeply, straighten my shoulders, and off we head for the broom closet.

Chapter Three :

The Big Break-Up

« So THAT's a Flemish Giant ? » Suze squints at the little furball in my hands. « You must be joking. This thing will easily fit inside an envelope. Maybe you can return it over mail-order. », she laughs at her own joke.

But I don't think it's funny. This is my New Best Friend, and it hurts a little. I secretly wish she would leave now.

Which, of course, she doesn't. She considers Furball a little longer and then suddenly looks up at me, as if struck by lightning.
« You broke up with him, didn't you ? » she

utters. « That's what this rabbit thing is, isn't it ? You're trying to get over him. Dear me, why didn't you tell me? I could have helped you with this, you know ...» She puts a reassuring hand on my shoulder.

Perplexed, I stare at her. I did not see this coming.
« No, no, Vian and I are fine... » I start off hesitantly, but then she shoots me a fierce « don't give me any nonsense »-look and my voice stops in midair. So, there it is. Time for Plan B. : we've moved to The Big Break-Up.

Although carefully rehearsed, my story somehow lacks conviction now I say it out loud. With a slight shiver in my voice, I sadly conjure up a boyfriend with more interests then are good for him (and me), resulting in endless waiting on my side for him to come home. I also tell her about the frustration of being abandoned during his endless trips to countries far and away. And then, as a bolt of lightning, the appearance of His Mistress.

A true Bohemian, the temptress that had stolen my One and Only had slowly ensnared his senses and had entranced him into leaving his love nest with me for a life of adventure and mind-blowing experiences. It was the letter in his pocket that had informed me of this passionate love affair. A letter which (and here I shed a little tear) made it clear to me that I could never have his heart again. I wring my hands at this point and give Suze a forlorn look.

« The nitwit ! », she cries out. « I knew it ! That inhuman hog didn't reach up to your kneecaps ! Oh, I saw this coming, all right. Artistic mumbo-jumbo ! He was out to conquer a string of women and then drop them like ordinary teatowels. Why didn't I warn you ? Why ? », she cries out to the heavens.

My mouth slightly drops. Really ? Three minutes ago she was going to marry me off to him, and now she says he's a right piece of codswallop and that she saw it all coming. I make a mental note to myself never to trust her opinion on my love life again.

Meanwhile, Furball, whom I had carefully placed on top of the kitchen table, and who had all along been patiently listening to our conversation, had decided he'd had enough, and tried to make a go for it. Alas, in mid-hop, Suze, always alert to everything, catches him by the skin of his neck and dangles him in front of my nose.

« Now this thing ! » she thunders.

« You're not seriously intending to keep it, are you ? You can't be that desperate ? What you need is a new boyfriend, not something that eats the furniture. Get rid of it now ! » she bellows. « Before I do !»

The very second she spoke those words, the rabbit started to shiver and then, with a « plop », vanished in a puff of smoke. We both stared, mystified, at the empty spot it had left behind.
I, of course, had been previously acquainted with the rabbit's uncanny ability to disappear. But Suze, dear Suze, had not. She just stood there, frozen to the spot. Her eyes were bulging and her tongue seemed to be tied in a knot. Very unlike her. It took her a while before she could speak again.

Then, she turned to face me and said, in her strictest manner, as if I were to blame for the whole thing :
« Where did you put it ? »
« I didn't put it anywhere .», I confess. « It went all by itself. »
« Rubbish . » Suze glares at me. « It's a trick, isn't it ? I'm trying to help you on your feet again, and all you can do is play a prank on me ? How utterly thoughtless! »

She turns and heads for the door.

« I'm leaving now. », she says. « And I won't be coming back until that critter is gone for good and you have found yourself a new man. Goodbye. » She turned her heels and headed for the door.

Phew. She´s gone. I sigh a sigh of relief. I never thought I'd see Suze in such a state. She'll come round soon enough, I think, she's far too curious to stay out of my love life. I'm guessing that she'll be at my doorstep within two days, begging me to go on a date with someone or other she's just met.

Anyway, it's a good thing she left. Now I can concentrate on Furball. Speaking of which, where on earth did he go ? He can't just have disappeared into thin air, can he now ? I open all the kitchen drawers. Nope, no Furball in sight. I look under the table, behind the flowers on the window sill and even inside the coffee pot. Still no rabbit. I sigh and sit down. Where could he be ? I look around the kitchen one more time and...hello ? What is that over there, in the corner ? A doormat ? With two rabbit ears and a bunny tail sticking out of it ? I get up for a closer inspection. I never owned a doormat in my life. And this one is twitching. I decide to touch it with my foot. And, with another « plop », Furball springs back to life, coughing up a hairball of what seems to be doormat straw.

I pick him up and carry him with me to the dining room. He's looking at me with a dull expression, as if to say : « I do this every day, you know, for a living. » I put him down on the chair. How on earth did a magic rabbit find its way to the pet shop around the corner ? Well, only one way to find out. I'll have to go over there and ask. So I put on my jacket and off we go.

Chapter Four :

The Back Door

      Ten minutes later I'm standing inside
the pet shop again. There is a long queue in

front of me, so I break out and take some time to look at the other rabbits. They all look fairly normal to me, minding their own rabbit business. No funny doormats in sight. Strange. Furball seems to be the only one around with magical powers. There must be a good reason why he ended up here.

When it's finally my turn, I put my box with Furball in it on the counter and address the shop keeper with an air of extreme gravity. « There seems to be something odd about my rabbit. » I confide in her.
She flashes me a smile.
« Returns are dealt with at the back of the shop. My collegue will be with you shortly. », she says, pointing me in the direction of another counter. « Next ! » she yells out to the customer behind me.
« No, you don't understand ! » I whisper urgently. « I don't wish to return it. I just have a few questions to ask you. »
She flashes me another smile.
« Everything is explained in the leaflet. » she states. « Just read it through. Next !»
« No, it doesn't. », I hiss through my teeth. « It doesn't come close to explaining what this rabbit does. »
« Oh, well then, not to worry, we have the full-size Rodent Encyclopaedia for sale. Only £59, 95. It's over there, in the corner. »

« No ! » I get hold of her arm now, before she gets a chance to yell « Next ! ».

« You don't understand. This rabbit is special . I need to know where it came from. »

« Oh, you need the breeders' catalogue ! » she rolls her eyes at me. « You should have said that first thing. All right, just give me a second. » She starts rummaging in one of the drawers. « I'm sure it's here. », I hear her mutter. « Where did it go ? Oh, yes, there it is ! » She hands me a list of names and addresses. « There you have them all. »

Forlornly, I look at the succession of names.

« But which of these homes does MY rabbit come from ? », I want to know.

« Couldn't tell you, sorry. » she smiles apologetically this time. « Just give them all a call and find out yourself. I'm a bit busy now, as you can see. Next ! » she calls out, this time with a certain finality to it.

I give up. The girl obviously has no clue as to what I'm holding in my hands. It seems there is nothing else to do as to call the entire list of breeders. Well, I have time on my hands, anyway. It's weekend, after all.

So, box in hand, I head back to my apartment. On the way over there, however, I notice my shoelaces are undone, on both shoes at the same time. Funny. This has never happened to me before. I bend down and put the box on the sidewalk next to me. I quickly tie up my laces and grab for the box again. But, failing to feel anything at all, I have to look over to where the box should be. And, lo and behold, it has disappeared.

« Oh, no. » I grunt. « Not again. »

This rabbit is proving to be a real escape artist.

I carefully scan the area. No streetlights with bunny ears. No strangely hopping dogs. Where on earth has Furball disappeared to ? And just then, I feel a slight prickling in my neck. I swiftly turn around and see a man is watching me. He does seem a little curious, although, at first sight, I fail to put a finger on what exactly it is that makes him stand out. Then it strikes me. He has two huge front teeth and pointy ears. And he´s holding my box.

« Aha ! », I think, » That's probably the owner ! » and I head towards him. But as soon as he sees I'm coming for him, he turns around and starts to walk away.

« Wait ! » I yell at him, but he takes no heed and continues. I fasten my pace in order to catch up with him, but no matter how fast I think I'm going, I can't seem to get to him.Then, suddenly, he turns the corner and I loose him out of sight.

I break into a run, but as soon as I turn the corner, I can see he has disappeared. Shoot. I look down the dark and empty alleyway. There are a lot of shabby-looking back doors, which all look thoroughly locked. One of the doors, however, has a very old rusty sign hanging out from it. It says « Authorized personnel only. ». Curious as ever, I draw a little closer. The door seems locked, so I take a look around, making sure no-one sees me, and then carefully remove one of my hairpins to pick the lock. Yes, a have learnt a few useful things in my days at college, and yes, I need hairpins to control the bird's nest on my head that is supposed to pass for a hairdo.

The door opens with a click. Carefully, I crane my neck inside. It's dark in there, but I can see a light shimmering in the back. I open up a little more and step inside. Suddenly, I hear a bird screaming at the top of its lungs. Before I have time to turn around and leave, a door in the back opens and a light is switched on. Feeling caught, I freeze to the spot.

« Who is this ? », a man barks at me. I blink into the light, trying to come up with a valid answer. But I'm dumbstruck.
The man quickly paces towards me. He is

huge, red-faced and dark-haired, and looks threateningly at me. I take a step back, just in case.

« This area is restricted. », he bellows. « Didn't you read the sign ? »

« Yes... », I finally manage to say. « I did. »

« So, what are you doing here? » he says, rather viciously.

« I am...lost. », I decide to say, « Someone took my rabbit and I thought he just might have gone in here. But I see I'm mistaken. I'll just go then, shall I ?» I quickly turn around.

« No, wait ! » the man's tone falls dramatically. « Your rabbit, you say ? », he whispers, « Just close the door, will you ? » I obediently do so.

« What kind of rabbit ? », he asks, taking a closer look at me.

« Just a small, fluffy, white one. », I say.

« Right. », he says. Then, after a short pause, « Would that rabbit happen to be a Flemish Giant ? »

« Yes, that's the one ! », I light up, happy that I've come to the right address after all.

The man grabs me by the sleeve. « Over here. », he says, and leads me a little further in the back. We pass the door he came in from, and with a small shock I realize that this is the backroom of the pet shop. We stop in front of a giant curtain, similar to the ones you see in theatres, and hands me a pair of headphones.

« Put these on . », he says. « You'll need them. », and with a large gesture he opens the curtain.

Suddenly, all hell breaks loose. The whole room is hissing, howling, shrieking and trumpetting at me, and I suddenly realize that the headphones he gave me don't even begin to cover up the racket that thunders on around me.

I stop and look around me, and I have to draw a sharp breath. A wild variety of the most curious animals I've ever seen is staring right back at me. They are obviously not used to visitors, since the racket they're making carries on and on.
And it's not just the noise. As we walk past the cages, I have to hold a hand in front of my nose, because the smell is, frankly, overwhelming.

« Here we are. », the man says, stopping in front of a glass cage. I can see Furball in it, all cooped up and sleeping tightly, oblivious to all the fuss around him.
« That's my rabbit ! » I say and tap on the glass in order to wake him.
« Don't ! » the man cries. « Let him sleep. He was exhausted when he came back. What did

you do to him ? »

A little miffed, I say : « Nothing. He just kept... disappearing all the time. »

« Ah, yes. He does that, doesn't he ? », he gives me a knowing smile. Then, « Did you feed him anything ? »

« No... », I say guiltily, realizing that I oversaw an essential part of basic pet keeping.

« Oh, thank God ! », the man blurts out. « So, there's no contamination there . »

« Contamination ? What do you mean ? » I'm baffled.

« Well, he's been out into the real world, hasn't he ? Who knows what bacteria he's been exposed to. That's why we have to keep him in quarantaine, you see. We can't risk it, with all the other animals about. Even the smallest bug could wipe them all out. »

Confused, I take a look around. None of the creatures in this room make any sense.

« So... what kind of animals are they ? », I venture carefully.

« Well, they're all very rare specimens. We found most of them in nature, but some of them I created myself. This one, for example... », he leads me to an acquarium, « ...is a Pigfish. I look at it in awe. With the snout of a pig and the body of an ordinary fish, the curiosity is happily splashing around the fish tank. How it breathes under water is a mystery to me, but it clearly works out well, since it keeps blowing out bubbles. I gape at it.

Then, the man points to the back of the acquarium, where I can discern another strange creature. It is trying to lift up from the bottom of the tank, but, loosing the battle, it decides to just stay put.

« This is Shelly, our Sheepodile. She's part sheep, part crocodile. We haven't perfected her yet, as you can see. »
« What's wrong with her ? »
« Well, she can't swim. That's because of the wool, you see. It weighs her down. We have to treat her with water-resistant hair products every day, or she sinks »
« Aha. », I nod, pretending to understand.
 « These aquatic creatures are just made for fun, though. The rest of the animals, however, were used especially for the circus. »
« The circus ? », I reply. « What kind of circus ? »
« Oh, you know, the usual kind, the one that travels around. » He doesn't expand on the subject, and I don't ask.

He leads me to a cage next to the acquarium. Inside it, a horse the size of a dog, with pink tufts along its back, is chewing on a bone.

« This is Paddy, our Poodlicorn, a cross between a poodle and a unicorn. », the man proudly announces. « The best act we ever had, if I may say so. The kids loved him, but he got grumpy whenever they wanted to take pictures with him. We had to refund several people for damage done to their trousers. He won't let go, you see, once he gets a grip. Cost us a fortune. »
I stay silent at this, not quite sure how to react to the idea of a raging poodlicorn.

« And this... », he leads me to another cage, « ...is Snuffles, the Flygaroo. As you can see, he is a cross between a flying fish and a kangaroo. He can jump over both our heads and land safely on the other side of the room. Great for acts with acrobats. Whenever they fall next to the net, he's always there to catch them. Good boy ! »

He fondly pets the animal's head and extracts what looks like fish pellets from his pockets. Snuffles happily chews away on them, then hops to the back of his cage and starts hugging a moth-ridden matrass with springs hanging out of it.

Seeing my surprise, the man explains :
« It's mating season. The matrass is the closest

thing to a female we could find. He seems happy enough, though, but we dread the day he finds out the matrass isn't producing any offspring. »

We continue to the next cage. It is enormous, and something huge and lumpy is staring back at us.

« This is Camelia, our Camelphant. », the man sighs. « Sad story, that. With her five humps she needs to drink every other hour. We had to give her twenty buckets of water before every show. Unfortunately, the stable boy forgot one day. Next thing you know, our poor girl here bursts into the crowd, waving her trunk, going for everyone's soft drink. We had to close down the circus after that. » He looks at me sadly.

« Oh. », I say, as I try to imagine the scene. « After that, we had to go into hiding. We were afraid the authorities would catch up with us. They would have put them all down, you know, every single one of them. Fear is a powerful thing, and our animals are rather prone to do, well... the unexpected. » He stops and thoughtfully runs his hand through his hair.

« So, we moved around the country... », he

continues, « ... finding abandoned buildings, empty ship yards, even a container park at one point. We never stayed long, three months at the most. Until we found this place. The manager of the shop is an old friend of mine. He was kind enough to lend us his back room. But we've been here for a whole year now, and it's getting cramped. The animals need fresh air, you know. »

« Do you mean to say that they never go outside? », I ask, a little apalled.
« No, never. And they miss it dearly. » He sighs. « If only I could take them all to Paradise Island. », he adds dreamily. « There's plenty of space there for all of them. »
« Paradise Island ? Where's that ? », I ask, intrigued.
«Oh, it's a little island off the coast. You won't find it on the map, though. It's protected. We don't want anyone to find out, you see? »
« Find out what? » , I want to know.
« How special our animals are. We have an enormous selection of fantastical creatures over there. We wanted to see what would happen if they mated with each other in the wild. And it exceeded our hopes. Every day, a variety of new species is being born, and they are all perfectly capable of surviving on their own. Well, we have to help them, occasionally, when the need arises, but that's basically it. »

« So, they're all free to go wherever they want? », I ask, a little shaken by the thought of meeting Camelia out in the open.

« Yes, they are. But, of course, they're not allowed off the island. There's no knowing what unspeakable things could happen to them if they fell into the wrong hands. On top of that, we make sure that Paradise Island is never discovered. We keep it off the radar. Not even satellites can see it. It's all done in order to make sure that the animals are protected from the gruesome bunch people can be. Safari hunters, for a start. They would love to see a Camelphant hanging from their walls. Then there's the government, as I told you. We want to keep our animals well away from them, since they consider them a threat to national security. » He sighs again.

« And then, worst of all, there are the tourists. »

« The tourists ? »

« Yes, the tourists. It starts with them nosing around a bit, seeing if they can feed the animals chewing gum, and it ends with an unfortunate incident that leads them straight into hospital and us into the arms of their lawyers. » He sniffs with contempt.

I think for a while.

« So...who IS allowed on the island, then ? », I carefully ask.

« No-one but Wagner, my companion, whom you've met on the street, myself, and a bunch of other people we met through the circus. We all have special qualifications. There is a doctor, in case one of them is ill. There is a trained nurse, who can take care of the newborns in case the mother dies. We also have someone who makes sure the animals don't make it off the island. As I said, we don't wish to be discovered. » He frowns.

« Then there's me. I oversee the whole breeding procedure and make sure they don't get hurt in the process. Some of the males can be a little... well, let's say, overenthusiastic. There was this incident with Francis the Flostrich, you see.. »

« Wait a minute, what's a Flostrich ? », I interrupt.

« Oh, he's half flamingo, half ostrich. », he explains helpfully. « Well, anyway, he was trying to mate standing on one leg. Of course, being half ostrich, his weight couldn't carry him and he kept toppling over. He was in a really bad state when we found him. It took us four months to nurse him back to health. Poor thing. Fortunately, by the time he got better, the mating season was over and we could release him back into the wild. »

I listen to him, open-mouthed.

« So, what about Wagner ? », I ask. « What does he do ? »

« Ah, well... let's say he takes care of the really special creatures...», he trails off.

« You mean the magical ones. », I state, a bit surprised that I finally managed to say the M-word.

He looks at me with a smile. « Yes, I mean precisely those. »

« So, Wagner is a magician ? », I boldly ask.

« Yes, indeed. He trains only the very talented animals, though, like Furball. Wagner and him were a joint act at the circus, you know. They did the most amazing tricks together. But that's all in the past now. », he sighs.

So Furball did come from the circus, I think, and I try to imagine him and Wagner doing a disappearing act.

« Anyway, », the man leads me back to Furball's cage. « I don't have time to introduce you to all our fantastical creatures. « Plus, it's feeding hour. So, I'm afraid you'll have to say goodbye to Furball. », he smiles apologetically. « And then you'll have to go. I'm sure our little secret rests safe with you. Because, if not, I trust Wagner to find you. » he gives me a stern look.

I'm not sure how to react to this. What exactly would Wagner do to me if he found me ? I'm trying hard not to think of anything unpleasant.

« Just one more question. », I venture.

« Yes ? »

« How exactly did Furball end up in the pet shop , where just anyone could have bought him ? »

« Ah, yes. », he nods. « A truly unfortunate mishap, that. You know, ever since the circus closed down, Furball has been a bit...bored. He keeps disappearing all the time. In the beginning, we raised the alarm at every occasion, but after a while we realized we just had to find the doormat with the bunny ears . » He pauses. « In the end, however, we got a bit negligent. It took us a few days before we realized he had gone for good. And by then, it was too late. He had escaped to the pet shop and was already in your possession. »

« Oh. », I say. « But then, how did Wagner find me ? »

« Easy. After you came back to the pet shop today, the sales girl complained that she had been « rough-handled » by one of the customers, who wouldn't let go of her. Something about a rabbit that didn't comply to the specifications on the leaflet. She gave us your description, and I immediately sent Wagner after you. »

« Rough-handled ? », I say, a little grumpy. « I didn't rough-handle her, I just took her by the arm. »

« Well, that doesn't matter now, does it ? The girl is all right, and we have Furball safely back in our possession. Case closed. »

I think for a while. « Just one more thing. », I say.
« Yes ? »
« All your animals are crosses between different species. So, what exactly is Furball mixed with ? »
He looks at me with a stern expression.
« You'll never guess. » Then, tentatively :
« You know, his magical abilities, they come from somewhere. An ancient creature with powers beyond our own. Rebirth is one of them. Curing diseases is another. At the end of its life, it bursts into flames and then rises again from its own ashes. Do you know what I'm talking about ? »
« A phoenix ? », I gasp, vaguely remembering a story I had read as a child.
« Exactly. A phoenix. No-one knows what powers are stored inside Furball, apart from the doormat routine. But he's still very young, and there's plenty of time to find out. Now, if you'll excuse me, I have other matters to see to.» He gently ushers me back through the curtain and all the way to the door.

Suddenly, the bird I had heard on my way in starts to shriek again. I try to locate where the noise is coming from, but fail to do so.

« It's all right, Barry. », the man addresses the ceiling. « She's all good. You can sleep on. » Dumbfounded, I look up. There, hanging upside down from a steel bar, is a giant parrot. It immediately tucks his head under one of its wings and starts to snore.

« This is Barry, our Barrot. », the man explains.

« You mean parrot. », I say helpfully.

« No, I mean Barrot. », he insists. « He's half bat, half parrot. He's deaf as a dodo, but with his echoe-locating skills he can detect the slightest vibration in the air. He's the perfect anti-burglar system, so we always keep him close to the door. You never know who might break in and enter. », he playfully winks at me.

« But enough chitchat. », he continues. « I really have to get going now, so I'm afraid we have to part here. Should you wish to purchase another animal at the pet shop, a voucher will be waiting for you there. Have a nice day. »

He pushes me through the door and is about to close it, when I cry :

« Wait ! »

« What ? », he says, a little impatiently.

« I didn't get to say goodbye to Furball. »

I seem to have hit a nerve. The man looks me up and down, as if he's measuring me up for something.

« Tell you what, », he says. « Why don't you come back tomorrow at noon ? I'm sure Furball will be awake by then. And perhaps, just perhaps, you could help me out with something... »
« What with? », I ask, intrigued.
« We'll see, we'll see... », he mutters, and with that, he closes the door.

Chapter Five :

The Black Swan

I walk and I walk and I walk. After having left the back room of the pet shop, I just have to get some fresh air. Too many things to think about. So, I'm taking a stroll through town.

My mind can't seem to stop mulling about those poor animals I saw. It must be absolutely horrible for them to be cooped up inside a cage all day. I secretly wish I could do something to help. But what ? I don't know any abandoned car parks or forests, and if I ask anyone, I'm bound to be found out. And I have to keep this a secret, or Wagner will be after me.

So, what to do ? Paradise Island would, of course, be the perfect solution. But why haven't they transported the animals over there yet ? There must be a reason... I think it over, but after a while, I have to give up. It's probably lack of money, I decide. It must be expensive to get all the animals over there at the same time. And neither Wagner nor the man I talked to seemed very rich. Their clothes were definitely moth-stained and whithered. I'd have to find out more tomorrow.

I stop walking and look around. Oh dear. I have no clue whatsoever as to where I am. It's definitely not the high-end of town, judging by the worn-down buildings and the painted-over street signs. I pull my jacket a little closer and decide to head back. But which way is that ? I didn't pay any attention to where I was going. I just turned a few corners and now I'm here.

I sigh. There are no cars or people around, which means I can't ask anyone. So I decide to turn around and go back in a straight line, hoping I will end up in a part of town I'm more familiar with.

After twenty minutes, however, I'm cold and hungry and still nowhere recognisable. I secretly curse myself for not having any sense of direction. Anyone else would have read the stars, or at the very least know where the magnetic north lies. But I'm a city-dweller, and for some reason city-dwellers like me don't do that kind of thing. We know where the nearest pub lies, and where you can find expensive shoes, but that's about it. We are an abomination of nature, and proud of it. But out here, in this wasteland, my city-dwelling skills are nothing short of laughable.

After another twenty minutes of trying to get out of the dead zone, I start to panick. There is still no-one around, and my feet really hurt. I decide to sit down on an abandoned bench. While I rub my feet, I take a look around. Nothing.

Except... wait a minute... what's that over there, at the end of the street ? Is that a light ? I put my shoes back on and go find out. And yes, believe it or not, there's a door door there, from which emanates a sound of laughter. There's a sign outside, which reads « The Black Swan ». Oh, thank God ! It's a pub ! Civilisation at last ! I almost cry in relief.

Gratefully, I open the door and enter. A wave of warmth washes over me, and I see the place is packed with people. They're all drinking, eating and laughing merrily. Who would have thought, in a forlorn hole like this?

I suddenly remember I'm hungry, and I walk over to the bartender. He smiles pleasantly at me.

« So, what will the young lady have ? », he says, cheerfully.

I blush slightly at this remark, because, let's be honest, it's been a while since anyone called me a young lady, even if I´m only twenty-two.

« What are the specials of today ? », I ask meekly.

He points at the billboard behind him. It has three courses on it. I decide to have the pork roast with potatoes and a salad.

« Coming up ! », he smiles again and he gestures me over to a vacant corner.

I walk over to one of the tables and sit down. But just as I'm taking off my coat, a man sits down next to me. He's rather handsome and is wearing an expensive suit. He seems a little out of place here, everyone else being dressed casually.

Before I have time to say anything at all, he leans over to me and says :
« Pretend you know me. I'll explain in a second. »

Too surprised to react, I just stare at him. Quickly, he puts an arm around my shoulder, gives me a peck on the cheek and

says, a little too loud for comfort :
« Imagine you being here ! What are you up
to these days ?»

Still, I fail to react. I'm hungry, I'm
tired and I just want the strange man to go. But
he doesn't, and when I finally manage to
extract myself from his embrace and stand up
to leave for another table, he grabs me by the
hand and pulls me down again. I feel slightly
alarmed now, and I'm looking around for help.

« Listen, », he whispers urgently, « This is
really important. You cannot go back to that
pet shop tomorrow. It is vital that you stay at
home. We cannot have you jeopardise the
whole operation. »

I stare at him blankly. « What operation ? », I
finally ask.
« Paradise Island. », he says. « They're leaving
tomorrow, and they're counting on your help. »
I blink. How on earth does this man know
about Paradise Island ?
« Don't go. », he urges me. « I'm warning
you. »
Then, a little louder : « Very nice seeing you
again ! Say hello to your husband ! »
And, with that, he leaves me and walks out the
door.

Shellshocked, I remain at my table. What was that all about ? Who is this man and how did he find me ? He must have followed me, I think. Following me seems to be the national sport these days. But how did he know about Paradise Island ? Could it be true that Wagner and co. are headed there tomorrow ? And that they need my help ? Is that what the man at the pet shop wanted to ask me this afternoon ? My head is spinning with questions.

Luckily, my dish arrives, and I have no more time to think. I quickly eat everything, without even tasting it. I really feel like going home now, away from strange men in expensive suits and pubs in forgotten places. I pay and ask the bartender to get me a cab. Half an hour later, I'm home.

Well, if you can still call it home. My door is wide open, and the contents of my apartment are scattered all over the place. Great. A break-in. Just what I needed.

Before I have time to draw my breath, Suze has rushed over to me from next door. « Oh, dear me ! There you are ! », she fusses. « I thought something dreadful had happened to you ! Where have you been ? »
« You know... out.« , is all I manage to say.

The less she knows, the better, I think. We don't want the whole world to find out.

« I was so worried ! », she continues. « When I found your apartment in this state, and you missing, I didn't know what to do. » She starts to shake all over. « So I called the police. »
« You what ? », I hiss at her. « Why ? »
She looks at me, taken aback.
« Well, I didn't know where you were, did I now ? I thought they'd kidnapped you ! » She is starting to sob now, and I have to hand her my handkerchief.
« I didn't even HEAR anything ! » She is positively wailing now, and I can't help but feel a little sorry for her. Not hearing a burglary taking place is bad enough as it is for Suze, but not hearing one that happens right next door, is nothing less than torture. I carefully sit her down and say :
« There, there. »

« I told them everything, you know. », she continues. « About you breaking up with your boyfriend, and the rabbit and all that. »
« The rabbit ? », I say, a little sick with nerves. « What exactly did you tell them about him ? »
« Well, you know, that you got him to get over Vian, and that you bought this completely oversized cage... »
« Yes ? »

« … and that that rabbit of yours disappeared into thin air... », she adds, sniffing loudly.
Oh no. I close my eyes. She told them. Not good.

« So... how did they react ? », I want to know, secretly hoping they took her for a raving lunatic.
« Well, they were very interested, of course. Vanishing rabbits are no laughing matter. They even called in a specialist, at one point. »
« A specialist ? What kind of specialist ? », I ask, my breath stopping in my throat.
« Oh, I don't know... someone from the government, I guess. I think his badge said something like « Special Agent Forrester ». He said this case was all very hush hush, and then asked me all sorts of questions. A handsome man, he was. Exactly your type. I gave him your number. Well, you were missing, of course, that's why he needed the number, but one can live in hope. I'm sure you'd love to meet him, he was quite charming. »

Suddenly, something clicks inside my mind.
« This man... », I say, « … was he wearing a rather expensive suit ? »
« Yes, he was, as a matter of fact. », she beams at me. « I knew you'd be interested ! But don't judge by appearances, my dear, a nice suit

doesn't mean he's well-off. Although I can't blame you for going after another rich man. You were probably used to a certain standard of living with Vian. »

I look at her in despair. She's unbelievable, this one. Handing out my phone number to strange men in the hour of need. Will she ever learn ?

I take a deep breath and plough on.
« Was he dark-haired, clean shaven, and smelling of expensive cologne ? »
« Yes ! », she says, rather surprised. « How did you know ? »
I let her question hover in the air for a while, failing to come up with an appropriate response.
« Wait a minute... », Suze lights up like a candle. « … is he an ex-boyfriend ? »

I hesitate for a moment. This would certainly be the easiest way out. So I hang my head guiltily and say : « Yes, he is. »
« You little devil ! », she's absolutely beaming now. « I didn't know you had dated a Special Agent ! Why haven't you told me ? You know you can confide in me ! »
Poor thing. She really has no clue.

« Sorry, top secret, that. », I wink at her. « I

would have had to kill you if I'd told you. »
She laughs appreciatively.
« I knew you were up to no good in the old
days ! Dating men from the Secret Service,
what do you know ! Good thing you have me
now, to set you straight ! »
« Hello ! », I protest. « Didn't you just try to
hook me up with the exact same man? »
For a moment, she looks unsure. Then, she
says :
« Ah, yes, but I know a true gentleman when I
see one, and I'm sure he has matured since
your early dating days. He has this aura about
him. », she concludes, dreamily.

Incredible Suze. If only she knew. I
think back of the events earlier this evening
and of how little aura I had detected in Special
Agent Forrester. Not to mention his
ungentlemanly behaviour, warning me off like
that. I'm tempted to tell Suze everything, but I
know it would be unwise. So I shut my mouth
tightly and shift uncomfortably in my seat.

Picking up on this, Suze gets up and
says :
« Well, anyway, I have to get going. It's late
and I still have to feed Mrs. Whiskers. I'll help
you clean up in the morning. Night night. »,
she hugs me and walks to the door.
« And remember, if you feel troubled tonight,

you're welcome to ring at my door. For a cuppa and a chat, you know. », she winks at me and leaves.

I lean back into my chair and heave a sigh. Alone at last.

Chapter Six :

Paradise Island

I lie in bed and toss and turn. I simply cannot sleep. All I can think is : how am I going to warn the man in the pet shop ? I have to tell him about Special Agent Forrester, or we can kiss the animals goodbye. But how ? I don't have his phone number, and I'm probably being watched by the Secret Services as we speak. It will be simply impossible to go over there tomorrow.

But then I think of something. Something clever. Something that will fool them all. I smile contentedly and turn over for a few hours' sleep, remembering to put my alarm clock. I don't want to be late tomorrow.

There is a lot to do, after all.

I dream of weird animals trying to catch me, and by the time it's morning, I'm exhausted. I make myself a strong cup of coffee, and decide to whip into action. First, I clean up my apartment. All my belongings are still lying around, littering the floor. It takes me a little longer than expected. I had no idea I owned so many things. I suddenly feel like reminescing about everything I've bought over the years, but I pull myself together. There's simply no time.

Then, when all is done, I pull out my Special Trunk from under the bed. In it, I have stored about anything fun I have collected over the years. Comic books, confetti, a pouch that squirts water when I shake someone's hand.

From it, I extract a black wig and a granny dress, that I used once at a costume party. I put them into a carrier bag and leave the apartment through the front door. If someone is watching me, I want them to see and follow me.

I walk straight towards the italian restaurant two blocks away. I enter and check that no-one comes inside after me. Good. The people from the Secret Service, if they're there, will stay outside and expect me to leave the restaurant in about an hour or so. Which gives me plenty of time.

I order a drink and proceed to the ladies' room. There, I change into my granny disguise. It looks quite convincing, I notice in the mirror. Then, I open a window and climb outside. There's no-one around and I head straight for the pet shop.

When I get there, the back door is already open. Wagner is waiting for me, and quickly pulls me inside. He doesn't seem fazed at all by my unusual attire, and for a moment I doubt that I did a good enough job fooling the agents.

The man I talked to yesterday comes and joins us. His face is drawn and he keeps wringing his hands.

« It was very dangerous of you to come here. », he says. « You may have endangered the whole operation. »

« That's what the agent told me yesterday ! », I blurt out.

« We know. They were here this morning, asking questions at the pet shop. »

I secretly curse Suze for her blabbering. Look in how much trouble she got us.

« So... you are aware of the fact that the Secret Services know all about Paradise Island ? », I ask.

« Yes. That's why we're in a hurry. We have to get the animals out now, or the agents will come back and find us. », he says, even-faced.

« You're leaving now ? », I say, bewildered.

« Yes. We have a boat waiting at the harbour and the loading trucks should be here any minute. »

I pause for a second. Then, I pick up all my courage and say :

« Can I help ? »

He looks at me sternly, then says :

« I rather hoped you would say that. But I hope you do realize that once you get involved in this, there is no way back. If they catch us, we will most certainly go to prison. Are you ready to take that risk ? Because, if not, now is the time to leave. »

To my utter surprise, I hear myself say : « I'm in. »

The man takes one more look at me, then takes me to the back. The animals are already packed up in crates. There is no sound coming from them, so I guess they've all been sedated.

As quickly as we can, we move the

crates over to the door. We're hardly finished, when we hear a truck pulling up, then another one, and another one. We hoist everything up into the back of the lorries and get seated in the front. Within seconds, we're gone.

I've never felt so tense in my life. Not even that fatal day, when my mum asked me where I got those condoms from. I'm absolutely shivering with fear, and I'm obviously not covering it up well enough, because the man puts a reassuring hand on mine and says :
« It's okay now, the hard part is over. You can relax. »

But the thing is, I just can't. Adrenaline is coursing through my veins, and I feel myself throwing up a little. What if the Secret Services find us at the harbour ? They might be waiting for us there. The world is starting to spin around me and I have to close my eyes for a moment. The man smiles at me and hands me a cold drink. I slowly start to feel better.

After a one-hour-ride, we finally reach the harbour. Our ship is lying on the other side of the dock, safely tucked away from prying eyes. We get out and, with the same efficiency as before, start transferring the crates.
 There are three people on the look-out, but

no-one raises the alarm, and after we've finished, we all climb on board. The ship lifts anchor, and off we go.

Safe at last. Relieved, I find myself a place on deck where I can sit down and breathe. A little further down, the man from the shop is talking to what I assume is the captain.

« A million thanks, my friend. », I hear him say. « And at such short notice. I owe you one, no doubt about that. » The man shakes his hand and says :

« Any time, old chap, any time ! You know we all stick together ! »

They walk on, leaving me alone to look at the waves.

I seriously hope I won't get sea-sick, I've had enough commotion to last me a life-time.

So I just sit and stare at the horizon and think of all the wonderful things that lie ahead.

And you know what ? I just can't wait to get to Paradise Island.

Chapter Seven :

The Arrival

It is early in the morning when we arrive. The sun has just broken through the clouds, and a miraculous sight meets my eyes. There are giant rocks all along the coast of the island, from where the most fantastic birds are taking off for flight. Alongside the boat, dolphin-like creatures are playing around in the water, hailing us with the most bizarre-sounding cries.

I can see a huge waterfall descending from the top of the mountain that dominates the island. The most amazing lush plants are growing everywhere, and the beach is littered with animals that resemble sea-cows.

The boat docks at a wooden passageway. Blinded by the sunlight I get off the boat and look around. Some people are already waiting for us and help us fasten the boat tightly. Behind the beach, I can make out a road on which a series of camouflaged trucks are standing by.

The man from the pet shop, whom I've come to know as Levy, walks over to one of the men and starts making arrangements for transport. We safely unload the animals from the boat and carry them over to the vehicles. Before long, we are all on our way to what I believe is the Sanctuary, the operating quarters of Levy's companions. As far as I'm told, there should be an office, an animal hospital, a hatching area and an orphanage. I am quite amazed at how professional it all is. And I still can't believe I'm on Paradise Island now.

When we arrive at the Sanctuary, we unload our crates and haul them over to Bay nr. 3. Bay number 3 is an area where the animals can rest before they are released into the wild. It has both indoor and outdoor facilities, and I think of how much better they're off now, with nature all around them.

We start unpacking the animals from their crates, and it takes us well into the night. Most of the animals are still sedated, but a few are looking around in amazement. They don't recognize their surroundings, and they're shifting about nervously.

« It will take them a few days. », Levy says ; « But once they're released into the wild, they'll be over the moon. I should have brought them here ages ago. »
« So, why didn't you ? », I ask, curious as ever.
« We were afraid af being discovered. So many trucks in one go are bound to attract the wrong kind of attention. And the Secret services have been after us since day 1. We had to be very careful.
But this time, we didn't have a choice. If we hadn't left immediately, they would have found

us. It was a close call, when they came to the pet shop the other day. If they had known we were hiding in the back room, they would have cleared us out straight away. »

« I'm not so sure... », I say, hesitantly.

« Why not ? », he asks, rather surprised.

« Well, this Special Agent Forrester I told you about... »

« Yes ? »

« Well, he knew I'd been talking to you the day before we left. He warned me off, and said not to contact you anymore. So, if he knew where you were, why didn't the Secret Services round you up straight away ? »

« Ah. I see. Good point. », he says, eyeing me closely. Then, bowing over to me, he says :

« Can you keep a secret ? »

« Yes, of course. », I say.

« He's one of us. »

« What ? », I almost choke. « Special Agent Forrester is on your side ? »

« Yes. We infiltrated the secret Services some time ago. Our friend Forrester kept an eye out for us, so we could be warned in time in case his colleagues found us. And find us they did, thanks to your nosy neighbour. »

« Suze. », I say, forlorny. « I'm so sorry about that. »

« It's not your fault. We shouldn't have ransacked your apartment. »

I look at him in utter amazement. « YOU

broke into my apartment ? But why ? »
« We had to make sure you weren't on the wrong side. You knew more about Furball than was good for you, and I had told you about Paradise Island. So, we raided your apartment to make sure you were clean. Then we made sure Forrester took over your friend Suze's call from his colleagues, and with this information we could trace your phone to The Black Swan. Speaking of, you'd better stay away from that part of town. Even Forrester wasn't happy to go there, and he carries a gun. »

I shiver. The man was carrying a gun and I didn't know. I'll never let strange men sit at my table again. Except, of course, if they're really cute.

It's late now, so we quickly grab something to eat and then Levy leads us to the living quarters. There are three enormous tents, one sleeping barrack for the men, one for the women, and one for sanitary use. We go to the women's quarters and Levy shows me my bunk bed. After such a long day, I am absolutely thrilled to find something soft to crash upon. Levy hands me a pair of pyjama's and some toothpaste, and explains I will find everything else in the shower room.

When he leaves, I feel grateful that the

day has gone by so smoothly. I lie down on my bed and think of all the events I have just been through. The ship, the unloading of the creatures and the visit of the Sanctuary. Before I have time to take a shower, I fall asleep, dreaming of what Paradise Island has in store for me tomorrow. Heaven knows what animals I will get to meet then. The adventure has only just begun.

Chapter Eight

The Sanctuary

It's already quite late in the morning when I get up. I'm the only one left in the sleeping quarters, so I presume that the others are already at work. I shower quickly and go over to Bay number 3. Wagner is already waiting for me at the entrance. With a spring in his walk, he guides me inside. He looks happy and relaxed, and without his usual shabby attire (he's wearing a blue-striped zookeeper's uniform) he could almost pass for handsome. Except for the hump in his back, that is. It's a good thing Suze is already taken, or I would introduce him to her.

For those who ask, Suze is in the

middle of a long-distance relationship with a sailor. He's overseas most of the time, and on the rare occasions he's home, he prefers the local pub over Suze's company. It drives her crazy, but for some reason she refuses to acknowledge the problem and talk him into staying with her permanently. Curiously, although she can be quite bossy towards her friends, Suze is a little poodle when it comes to her relationship to Alfred. He seems to wear the slippers at home.

Which explains why Suze puts all her energy into my love life, her own being so miserable. But the day she breaks free of Alfred, I will definitely pass her Wagner's phone number. I haven't quite forgiven her yet for handing out my number to Special Agent Forrester.

Levy joins us and he too is positively bubbling with good spirits. He leads me to the cantine, where I enjoy a hearty breakfast. The omelet tastes a little strange, though, as if there's too much yolk in it. But I wolfe it down all the same. Travelling makes you hungry.

Levy, who has joined me in eating the omelet, then asks me if I would like to go on the Grand Tour of the animal lodgings. Would I ? Of course I would ! So, we head off to the outdoor facilities first.

Here, the biggest and most dangerous of the animals are kept behind fences. The patch of land allotted to each one of them is roughly ten times the size of a normal zoo. There's plenty of space for all of them. I can see some large creatures grazing peacefully in the sunshine. One of them is Camelia, the camelphant. She looks thoroughly satisfied with her new surroundings and behaves as if she's always belonged here. I can see there is a pond a litlle further on, where she can drink all she wants. I really feel happy for her, and almost feel like cuddling her. Almost. Because, unfortunately, the coward in me recoils from coming within ten metres of animals that are bigger than myself. I think I've seen one too many dinosaur movies.

We walk on and Levy shows me a herd of the most bizarre creatures I have ever seen. They are chicows, he tells me. They look like cows but they have feathers like a chicken and, believe it or not, they lay eggs.
« It's a huge success ! », he tells me , « We can feed our staff for one week with just one egg ! The omelets are fabulous ! I believe you just had one for breakfast. Didn't it taste great ? »
I give him a shy smile. I'm not about to break his enthusiasm. I'm a guest here, after all.

« We try to eat as little meat as possible, you see. » he continues, « Only the animals which die of natural causes end on the menu. But on the whole, we live like vegetarians. I hope you understand. You can't deal with animals all day and then have them for dinner.»

I nod in agreement, because I am already part of the vegetarian wave. It is, after all, one of the reasons why I got Furball instead of a snake, Furball being a co-vegetarian. My only sin is bacon. As long as they serve it, I simply have to have it.

Levy has moved on to the next patch. « This one, », he points at a cow with enormous horns, « was also bred for culinary reasons. We call her Chocolate Moose. She is half cow, half moose. Her mother was a brown cow, and , as you know, brown cows make chocolate milk. We crossed her with an ordinary moose and bang ! There was our Chocolate Moose. Her milk is even frothier than her mother's, but we still haven't figured out how to eliminate the typical musky flavour that emanates from it. Our lab is working on it, though. We're expecting a breakthrough any day now. » He smiles contentedly.

We walk past a patch of land with extra-high fences. I immediately guess this is the predator area. In the back, I can see a couple of animals lying in the shadow of a huge tree. Levy explains they are ante-leopards. They are the unhappy result of a bet between Levy and the other men. They had been argueing about which animal was the fastest : the antelope or the leopard. Levy had won the bet by saying it was the leopard, since it can catch the antelope. But this got their minds going and on a drunk afternoon they decided to cross both species in order to see if their new creature could go twice as fast as a leopard. They made three of them, but it turned out that one was lazier than the other, so the project was abandoned.

« We've never seen them run. », Levy shakes his head. « We even have to hand-feed them. They just won't bother getting up for fresh meat. They're an absolute disgrace. » He sighs deeply.

I feel a little sorry for him. Some of his projects seem to go wrong, and I secretly wonder how many animals have suffered from cross-breeding failures. I decide to ask him politely.

« So... how long have you been creating animals for? », I venture, still staying on the safe side.

« All in all ? I guess I started in my twenties. My first attempt was a dragonfly. The scientist

community looked down on it, but as far as I know, you can still find them today. »
« The dragonfly was your invention ? », I ask, baffled.
« Yes, of course. Then came the clownfish, and it was just uphill from there on. »
I have a hard time hiding my amazement.
« So ...you released some of your creations in nature ? »
« Oh, yes. The catfish, for instance. And the bulldog. Huge successes, both of them. But we had to stop somewhere. If you mess with nature, it can backfire. You never know what can happen if our animals breed with other species. So we decided to use them for the circus instead. Much safer. Until we found Paradise Island, that is. Here we can breed freely. The island belongs to a friend of mine, who bought it for next to nothing from the government. We can do whatever we like here, as long as no-one finds out. As far as I know, this is the only place on earth with a breeding program like ours. We are unique, and we intend to keep it that way. »

I nod. But there is still one question that's bothering me.
« So... », I pause, « did you ever make a creature that was severely handicapped, or, worse, not fit to live ? »
He looks me up and down. I can see he had not

expected this.

« It happens. But most of our animals are the result of months of planning and testing. We don't take any risks. And once the DNA-sequence fits together, there is not much that can go wrong. Although some of our creations have really strange personality quirks. The menguins, for instance. »

« The menguins ? »

« Yes. We should never have made them. They are half man, half penguin. They look like the birds you know, but they have arms and legs. We thought they would use their hands for tool-making, but instead, they just keep pushing each other over. It's like watching a game of bowling with live pins. Hilarious, really, but we have to hospitalize them all the time. A real shame, they would have been very popular at the circus. »

I try to imagine his menguins for a while. But then another question pops to mind.

« Don't their feet freeze to the ice ? »

« Yes, they do. That's why we provided them with shoes. It took us ages to show them how to tie their laces, though. It's like teaching three-year-olds. And now, of course, their favourite prank is to tie each others laces together. It's a huge mess. Our medical team keeps working around the clock. And then, of course, there are the eggs. »

« The eggs ? »
« Yes. The menguins play football with them.
It's their favourite afternoon activity. We
should never have given them those
sneakers. »
« So, what happens to the eggs ? », I wonder
out loud. « Do they survive ? »
« Well, in the beginning we tried to save some
of them. But, in the end, we had to give up.
The little menguins were horrible creatures,
pulling each other's feathers out and biting
each other in the toes. So we decided to just let
them die out naturally. »

I stare at him in shock. « So, not all
animals make it in the long run ? », I ask.
« Well, we try to copy a natural habitat. If they
can't survive on their own, we havei to let
them go. It's tough, but nature can be cruel
sometimes, and we don't want to play God.
There is a natural balance to everything, and it
is important to keep it that way.»

I think about this for a while and, since
thinking always makes me a bit depressed, I
start to grow a little darker. Fortunately, Levy
picks up on my mood and grabs me by the
hand.
« Don't worry about this now. You should be
enjoying your stay here. If you're up to it, I can
show you the indoor facilities now. »

« Yes, I would love that. », I say, relieved to break away from my musings, and follow him inside.

He leads me to the reptilian section first. All the animals are safely tucked away behind glass. I can see trees and plants which remind me of a tropical rainforest. Exotic flowers and berries are competing with each other, and there are a lot of insects buzzing around. Levy points to a few snakes hiding on the branches and lazing in the warmth. They are really hard to spot. With a pang, I am reminded of the snakes at the pet shop. And of Furball. I had almost completely forgotten about him. I'll have to ask Levy about him later on. But for now, my attention is caught by an altogether different animal.It seems to be covered in all the colours of the rainbow at the same time. Levy explains that this is the camelion. The size of a small lion, it is suppose to adapt to the colours of its environment. But it seems to be failing miserably.

« We don't know what's wrong with it. When it blends in with the colours of the trees, it can catch all kinds of insects and feed. But with this attirement, it will probably die very soon. A pity, it could have made a fortune at the circus. », he sighs.

Seeing his despair, I try to console him. « Maybe one day, you can start up with a circus again. », I say, light-heartedly. « You might be able to get the government to approve of the small animals. You'll just have to leave the big and dangerous ones out. »
« Yes, maybe », he says. « But we'll have to prove to them that we treat our circus animals well, which we do, of course. Unfortunately, the government administration lacks the appropriate forms to describe the blend of animals we provide, which leads to a bureacratic nightmare. It will take years before we can get them into the system. And by then, new animals will have surfaced and we can start all over again. It's a fight we cannot win. »

« But can't you convince some politicians to find a loophole in the laws they make every day ? »
« Yes, we can, if we open a school where children can learn about the pros and cons of animal breeding. Playing around with DNA is still at its first stage, and we need to show the children of this planet the dangers of messing about. We cannot be careful enough. »
« But that's a brilliant idea ! A school would be perfect, and Paradise Island is the ultimate place for children to visit. »

« You'd think so. », Levy shrugs. « But the island is, unfortunately, a hazard to all who come across it. Securing the island would cost us a fortune, and the people who work here have no degree in either breeding or security. We work from experience only, and attracting DNA and security specialists is out of our reach. We simply do not have the funds. »
« Is that what's bothering you ?. », I say, « Funds ? »
« Well...yes...isn't that important ? »
« Not for me ! », I smile gently at him. « Give me twenty-four hours. You won't regret this, I promise you ! », and I leave him for the nearest phone.

A few calls later, I have successfully managed to convince my boss to invest in the Paradise Island School Project. Our company is always supporting the arts and education projects, and my boss was wild with the idea of being the only one involved in this. Being a father himself, he adored the possibilities the island would offer for future generations, and being the first at providing a holiday camp in nature, with unknown species, tickled his imagination. Of course, he wanted to involve the press straight away, but I had to ask him to keep it quiet for a little while longer. Just until Levy and his people had OK'd the project, and agreed to give him the Grand Tour of the island. I couldn't wait to tell Levy.

But where was he ? I couldn't find him anywhere, and even the staff seemed perplexed at his   disappearance. I decided to find Wagner instead. He'd probably know where Levy had gone.

I find him at the cafeteria, carefully sipping on a cup of coffee. He looks dead-tired, as if he'd been up all night.
« It's the salmonsters. », he admits after my asking. « They've hatched. And there are way too many of them. We can't control them anymore. They're eating all the fish in the lake. We've been trying to catch them all night, but they bite through our nets and we've lost three rowing boats. Someone even lost a toe. It's a disaster. »

I'm afraid to ask what salmonsters are, but Wagner sees the question marks in my eyes and explains :
« The salmon we put out in the lake has bred with the local piranha's . We never thought this would happen, as the salmon was their food, not mating material. But what can you expect, on an island like this ? » He closes his eyes for a moment.
« What are we going to do ? », he continues.
« If we can't catch them, they will definitely

start to attack all the animals that drink from the lake. There are simply too many of them. We'll have to close off the whole area, and God knows how we're going to provide water for the animals, without the lake. We'll have to drive around with a fire truck or something and spray them with hoses. And give them plenty of water from all the buckets we have.» His shoulders have sloped and he's holding his head as if this is the end for him.

« It was my responsibility, the lake. », he says sadly. « They probably won't keep me on after this. Not unless I can find a solution, and fast. »

Great. I solve one problem, and there is the next. I will have to help Wagner figure this out, though, or the island will not be ready for my boss's visit next week . And everything depends on that. If he flunks the project, there go our funds.

So, I sit down next to Wagner, and we do some serious brainstorming. And, believe it or not, we come up with an excellent plan.

Chapter Nine :

Furball's change

A few hours later Wagner and I are standing by the lake. We've come up with a magnificent plan to catch the salmonsters. With the help of his team, Wagner has boosted up their only radio with gigantic speakers, the size you only see at concerts. Taller than a man, they are screwed up till full power. When we insert them into the lake, their self-made plastic coating not only protects from the water all around, but enhances the bass sound emanating from them. Five men are standing around the lake with rowing boats, ready for our sign. With a countdown from ten, we start up the radio at full blast. Within seconds, all the fish within the lake are stunned from the music and come floating up to the surface. All we have to do is catch the right ones and leave the rest alone. When they wake up from their paralysis, the other fish will just continue to swim on, and the salmonsters will be safely within the acquarium on the Sanctuary.

« Go ! » Wagner shouts, and the men aptly direct their boats towards the multitude of fish in the center of the lake. It takes us all afternoon to catch the salmonsters, and by the time the sun sets, we are off to our base. The salmonsters are still asleep, and when we arrive we safely tuck them into a freed space within the fish tank. Their area is fenced off, so they cannot attack any of the other species swimming around. Still sweating from the effort, we congratulate each other with the perfect outcome of our plan. It couldn't have gone better, and Wagner invites the crew to a drink in the bar.

Not feeling much for an alcoholised beverage myself, I decide to find out where Levy has gone to. He's still missing, and Wagner told me that he had no inkling as to where he might have gone. I search both the sleeping quarters and the hatching area, but to no avail. Tired and hungry, I decide to pay Furball a visit before heading off to the cafetaria for a bite. I haven't checked on him since our arrival, and I have to admit that I miss him a little.

When I arive at his cage, I see to my surprise that Levy is sitting next to it, fast asleep on a chair. His hair is a mess, and his clothes look like he's had a rough few hours. He looks like a lost man, sitting there all alone, and I choose to ignore his shabbyness. I carefully prick him on the shoulder. He wakes with a shock, and I can see he has dark circles around his eyes.

He stares back at me. It takes him a while to register who I am.

« Hello, sunshine ! », I greet him.
He gives me a look darker than the deepest abyss.
« Hello. », he mutters.
« What's up ? », I venture, but he simply doesn't answer.
A bit more worried now, I say : »Everything okay ? »
With a gloomy shake of the head, he sighs : « It's Furball. He's changing . »
« Changing ? », I ask, unsure of what he's referring to. As far as I know, Furball doesn't have any clothes, and for some reason he seems too young to go through menopause.
He sighs again. « You know we crossed him with a phoenix... », he continues.
« Yes ? »
« Well, there are complications . »
My breath stops. « What kind of complications ? », I ask.
« He's died three times now, but he can't seem

to get round to changing into a bird. The first time, he sprouted a bird's head, but kept a rabbit's body. The second time, it was the opposite way around. And now he seems to grow feathers in the most peculiar places, but has fur in his ears. I just don't know what to do with him. » He nods in despair. « The poor thing is completely at a loss as how to do this properly and I can't help him. All we can do is wait. »

I take a look inside the cage, and truthfully, Furball is a mess. He's looking at me with big beady eyes, and I can't help but feel sorry for him. Then suddenly, he flares up into a fireball again and disappears into ashes.

« He's speeding up », Levy says, all choked up. « If this doesn't stop, we'll have to put him down. It's more than we can expect of him. He's miserable. «
I look sadly at the pile of ashes he left behind. Poor thing. I can feel my throat narrowing and my nose is starting to run.

With a sudden pang, Furball comes back to life, and this time he is almost not recogniseable. With just one rabbit ear, and one paw, he looks more like a play-doh experiment gone awry than a liveable creature. He has feathers sticking out of his bottom and is yelping softly. My heart stops, and all I want to do is help him. Slowly, Levy takes him out of his cage and pats him softly. Furball closes his eyes in pure misery, as Levy cuddles him one last time.

« I can't do this to him anymore. », Levy says, with tears in his eyes. « I'll have to end this before he's in too much pain. He doesn't deserve this, and he's been so brave all day and night. It's all my fault, I shouldn't have messed with magical creatures, I have no expertise in the area. »
He slumps his shoulders.
« Goodbye, my friend, I'm so sorry...», he gently says and puts Furball on his chair. I see him grab his gun and change the stunning dart for a real bullet.

« Wait ! », I cry out, all panicked. « Just wait a little. Let me hold him one last time. I haven't had a chance to say goodbye yet.»
Tears are streaming down my face as well now, as I realise this is the end for my little companion.
Levy hands him over to me, and I carefully put him on my lap. Furball seems to relax a little, as I hold him in my hands. He is clearly exhausted. With a soft kiss, I say my farewell and put him back on my lap. I softly stroke him while Levy puts the gun to his head, ready

to pull the trigger.

But then something unusual happens. Furball starts to buzz slightly and a strange light emanates from him, as if he's changing into pure energy. A white ball of sizzling light suddenly lifts up from him and explodes right over us. By the time Levy and I can see again, a most beautiful bird is looking up at us. It is magnificent. Its feathery attire is made of the most bright colours, and the pearls in its eyes are shining brightly. I've never seen such a beautiful creature in my entire life, and realise this must be a phoenix.

Wagner is looking at it in shock.
« It was the kiss ! », he cries out, « Why didn't I think of this myself ? It was love ! He needed love ! And you gave him the purest love there is ! That's what cured him ! Oh, my God ! Thank you ! », he turns to me.
« You saved him ! », and this time I can see tears of gratefulness streaming down his cheeks.
« Thank you, thank, you ! », he repeats, and he gives me a gigantic hug.
« I thought Furball was history ! But you did it ! He's finally changed ! Let's hope he will stay like this now for a while, I can't see him change one more time, poor thing ! »

Then he puts his hand to his heart and says : « Anything. Anything at all. Just ask. This is worth anything in the world to me. Just tell we what you need and I'll do it for you. », he adds gravely.

I feel a pang of relief myself as I put Furball safely back into his cage. He starts to feed straight away on the bird seed that Levy had provided for him earlier. I look at him dearly. It seems I've saved the day. I'll have to stop rescuing animals, or they'll keep me on Paradise Island forever, and I'm starting to miss home a bit. Too much excitement in the last twenty-four hours, and I'm kind of missing my sofa and a strong cuppa. But before I go back home, there is one more thing I have to settle. So I sit Levy down and say :

« Actually, there IS something you can do for me. », and I start to explain.

Chapter Ten :

Zelda the Zippo

Levy is listening to me with open mouth. I just told him about my boss's visit next week and he's wildly enthusiastic. The Paradise Island School Project is on its way. All I need him to do, is to ready the island, and make sure all animals are safe and of no threat to their environment. That means the fences have to be double-checked, the lab and kitchen have to be upgraded to modern hygiene standards, and for the guided tour of the island we'll have to provide visitors with helmets and safety vests in case someone gets bitten, or, worse, eaten. The hospital will have to be equipped with first-aid kits, a room for immediate surgery, and plenty of consoling lollipops.

For the Grand Tour of the island, we'll have to get hold of a reinforced, stainless steel school bus which can take an attack or two, and, just like on wildlife trips, we'll equip the staff with stun guns in case some of the animals become too enthusiastic.

All this has to be ready by the time my boss arrives, and we'll have to make sure he has a good overview of what we have to offer modern-day school children.
Levy and I start making up a plan for the guided tour we would like to present to him.

On Day One, we'll start with the hatching area. We'll have to find some really cute and cuddly animals, preferably without teeth, which the children can pet and take care of. Then we'll go to the outdoor facilities of Bay number 3, where the kids will be allowed to feed the predators and take a ride on Camelia, the Camelphant.

Afterwards, we'll jump on the bus for the Grand Tour of the island. In case of rain, we have the indoor facilities of Bay number 3, where both the acquarium and the reptilian section will most certainly be a hit with the youngsters. Feeding the salmonsters is always quite spectacular, and gigantic Flyders, or flying spiders, are sure to extract a scream or two from even the most withered youth.

Then, in the afternoon, we'll all head off to the cafeteria, for some healthy, vegetarian-inspired food, which, apart from our freshly-grown vegetables, includes grilled insects and a selection of Chocolate Moose's dairy products, such as chocolate cheese and cacao. Those with food allergies will be taken care off separately.

Finally, it's time for the lab, where a course on the dangers of wild animal breeding will take place, after which everyone will be allowed to experiment freely.

Then it's back for another bite, and, before the kids go to bed, there will be a campfire out in the open with a storyteller specialised in mythological animals, like Pegasus, the flying horse, Centaurs, which are half man, half horse, Medusa, the goddess with a head full of snakes instead of hair, the Minotaur, which is half bull, half man, and so on.

For those who can't sleep after that, we'll provide hot water bottles and music with the soothing sounds of nature, like tropical bird songs and waterfalls. Levy tells me he has just the sound track for it, and swears you can even hear rainbows breaking through the rain. I blink for a second at this information, but know better than to disturb a man in his fantasies and let it go.

We are still in the middle of planning, when suddenly Levy's phone rings. There's another emergency. I see him listen with extreme gravity.
« Okay, I'll be there shortly. », he says, and hangs up.
« Looks like we're up for our first crisis of the day », he frowns. « Want to tag along ? »

I don't have to think twice. We hop into one of the jeeps, and Levy explains what happened on the way over. Zelda the Zippo is in a sorry state. Half hippo, but with the typical stripes of a zebra, she's been bathing in the local mud in order to get rid of the insects that plague her every day. The mud cures her wounds and she enjoys a mud bath now and again because it's so utterly relaxing. The problem is, the mud won't come off anymore, as there hasn't been much rain lately, and it has dried up in cracks on her skin. This prevents her from moving around freely, and she had been unable to feed properly.

As we arrive at the puddle where she dwells, we can see she's completely miserable. Her mouth is wide open in pain and a couple of vultures are cirkling around her, hoping she will crash to the ground any time soon. We have to do something. Levy is already radioing to his crew, asking them to send over a towing truck in order to get her to the animal hospital. While we're waiting, we take care of the most impressive wounds from the vulture attacks, but the bandage we took along doesn't seem big enough to cover her whole body.
« We'll need surgery. », Levy says, « And lots of stitches. »

When the towing truck arrives, we crane her up into the back. One of the crew offers to hose her down with water, so the mud will wash off, but Levy is afraid that it will get her blood flowing. She would suffer too much blood loss before we get to the hospital. So we leave things as they are, and Levy goes and sits in the back with her in order to calm her down.

When we arrive at the hospital, the rest of the crew is already stand-by. We carefully lift her off the truck, and immediately, a team of nurses starts to take care of the wounds. We ship Zelda off to the surgery area, and lay her on a huge canvas, where the specialist starts working on her right away. At this point, one of the nurses asks us to leave, which we do, and we head off to the cafeteria for a strong cuppa.

Levy looks tired, but happy.
« She'll come round soon enough. Just a couple of days at sick bay and she'll be right as rain. We did a good job today. », and he flashes me a smile. « Now let's get back to our planning, before anything else comes up. You never know what's next in this place, and we really need to get this done as quickly as possible. »

I smile at him and get hold of my papers.
« No problem, chief. », I give him the thumbs up. « We'll have this done before you can blink. »

Chapter Eleven :

The Golden Tooth

On Day Two, Levy and I agree the children should start with a healthy breakfast. Nothing better than sliced toast with jelly or cereal to get the brain going, and growing youngsters should never be underfed when attending classes, or bein led around a paradisial island with strange and fierce creatures in it, or accidents will happen.

Then, after some intensive brainstorming, Levy and I come up with the next step in our daily schedule. Following breakfast, our children will be allowed to choose one from five different morning activities :

- Those interested in zoo-keeping can give a hand in Bay number 3 and learn all about the quirks and feeding habits of our animals.

- Those interested in food can follow a specialised course in how to save the planet with tasty vegetarian dishes for human consumption.

- Those interested in medicine can follow a class on how to perform first-aid on a wide variety of our creatures. As some of those are in the possession of a healthy set of teeth, however, mouth-to-mouth will only be optional. If the occasion arises and a large animal comes into sick bay, our students will safely be set to the side and be encouraged to help, watch and learn from a distance.

- Those interested in nature can go on a survival camp and learn how to make a encampment, how to grow your own food and how to survive attacks from the surrounding wildlife, played by our staff. Safer is better, after all, and we don't want to risk anything.

- Those interested in the circus will be shown all the tricks of the trade and learn how to work next to, on top of and, in some cases, under our animals. We hope that the youngsters' enthusiasm will incite our politicians to open us up for circus travel again, or, at the very least, that they will let us put up a show or two on the island. I'm sure our Floodles, or flying poodles, would like to stretch their legs now and again.

Then, after a spot of lunch, we will continue with the afternoon activity, which is the same for everyone : a treasure hunt of formidable proportions. Through a series of exercices such as arrow-shooting, falcon-hunting, and Chicow-tipping, each team will have to search for the Golden Tooth, an elephant- like contraption, which we will hide in a cave somewhere. The winning team will be awarded free tickets to Paradise Island, so they can come back with their families and friends, and show them what an excellent place this is.

Finally, to conclude our event-filled weekend, we take our youths back to base camp, where we shoot some funny pictures of them in head-in-the-hole animal posters and give them a cuddly toy of one of their favourite creatures.

Levy and I lay down our pens. We are both exhausted after so much planning, yet thoroughly convinced that our tour will be a huge success. By the time my boss arrives, everything has to be airtight, though, and Levy and his crew will have a tough time getting everything done by next week. Of course, I will give them a hand, and, in my spare time, set up some contacts with the press to travel along, which Levy finally okayed. We're hoping they can break the story before we contact the schools. We'll sell Paradise Island as The Place To Be to help the animals of this planet, and hope that this will make the school boards' mouths water. All we'll have to do after that, is pick up the phone and take reservations. We'll be solid gold after that, and, over time, we might even have to build some sturdy holiday quarters instead of our basic sleeping tents. The sky's the limit.

I smile broadly and Levy looks at me. He puts a hand on my shoulder.
« Thanks for your help.», he says, with gratitude in his voice. « We couldn't have done this without you. »
I give him a solid smile back.
« You're welcome. », I say warmly, and in a confident tone, I add : « So from now on, don't you worry about a thing. We've got it all covered. If your staff does what they're supposed to, there is simply nothing that can go wrong. » And we toast to the future of Paradise Island.

Chapter Twelve :

The Visit

It's been a hard week. Levy, Wagner and the crew have been working in overdrive in order to get everything ready. We're all tired and grumpy, but we know our ordeal will be over soon. My boss will arrive any minute now, and a welcoming team has been sent out to the harbour. The press will arrive in the afternoon, in order to take a few shots of the island and, preferably, of my boss and Levy shaking hands. We will only have a few hours with them, as their schedule is filled up with other, more important stuff, like the president opening a new golf course, or some superstar getting their lips all botoxed-up. It's a sad world we live in.

So Levy and I are sitting around nervously, hoping that everything will go well. The animals are fed and calm, the security measures are in place, and the staff is all washed up and dressed in professional uniforms. The only tricky part is showing them the island itself, as the wildlife out there is largely unpredictable. Which is why we warned my boss to dress up in « casual » clothes. In our slang, that means that, if torn, they can easily be replaced by a T-shirt and a pair of jeans we have lying about. Our current budget does not include expensive costumes as yet.

Wagner comes in and gives us the OK-sign. My boss has safely arrived at the harbour and is on his way to the encampment. We get up, brush a few hairs of our uniforms, and go outside in order to greet him at the entrance. I have jitters in my stomach and my palms are cold and sweaty. For me, it's not only Paradise Island which is on the line, but my promotion as well. I was promised a position as head of the advertising team, and if my boss is unsatisfied, he will think twice as to put me in charge of anything whatsoever. Except maybe toilet-scrubbing. So, with shaky hands, I step outside.

Fortunately, the wait doesn't take long. After only a few minutes , I can see the jeep approaching. My boss gets out, and I cheerfully go over to him in order to bide him welcome. I introduce him to Levy, and we head off to the cafeteria for a nice hot beverage. My boss, who is definitely not the sea-faring kind, is inordinately happy to be able to sit down on a stable chair and hauls his tea inside him with conviction. We chat non-commitally about the weather, his trip, and the lottery ticket he purchased only this morning. He felt this could be his lucky day. Of course, we are not about to bereave him from that fantasy.

Finally, after a whole pot of tea for him and a whole lot of patience from us, we get up and show him around the facilities. He is wildly impressed by our professionalism, and, upon seeing our animals, behaves like a child in a candy shop. He wants to pet them all, and only Levy seems to be able to calm him down and talk him out of getting too close to the Flygers, or flying tigers.

Then comes the moment of truth. We hop into one of the vehicles, and drive him around the island. Upon seeing the wild variety of interbred animals, he is positively cooing. We let him out now and again, so he can take a closer look. He is absolutely gobsmacked by the gorraff, a crossing between a gorilla and a giraffe, and we literally have to drag him away from the liophants, which are half lion, half elephant. We take a few shots of him feeding them, and then carefully guide him back to safety. Luckily, everything goes well and Levy and I are beyond relief when we arrive back at our base. We go in for a bite to eat, while we wait for the press to arrive.

Levy and I lay out our plans for Day Two, which isn't up and running yet, since my boss has to leave the same day. He fully approves of our ideas, and can't wait to introduce his children to Paradise Island. Feeling the mood is right, Levy then takes the bull by the horns and switches over to our main topic of interest : money. After some pulling and towing, we get him to approve of our budget, and all is well in the world. The Paradise Island project is go.

That is, until the press arrives. Although I have had solid contacts with media people throughout my career, nothing had prepared me for what would come next : the journalists were not alone.

As some sort of media stunt, they had brought along a few actors, dressed up as prehistoric people with bear skins. They'd had a brilliant idea during a late-night brainstorm and were going to call our project « Our last chance to save the planet » . Nothing wrong with that, of course, except that they wanted us to round up a number of animals which would get the imagination of the public going, and which, of course, were all lethally dangerous. According to them, this would make for a spectacular-looking picture on the front page. The readers would, no doubt, lap it up and hop on the boat to Paradise Island straight away.

Now, I don't think I need to explain the gravity of the situation. The journalists were clearly not aware of the fact that dangerous wildlife does not mix very well with human flesh. Needless to say, we trashed their idea, and convinced them to settle for a picture of

Levy and my boss with a giant cheque, which we had prepared in advance.

Thinking back, I realise the journalists conceded a tat too easily. They took their pictures, scribbled down a few notes, turned down a tour of the island, and cheerfully said that they would would prefer to walk back to the boat, in order to get some fresh air. Relieved, we sent one of our staff along to guide them on their way, together with my boss , and that was that. We thought.

Half an hour later, Levy and I are merrily chatting along at the cafetaria, going over the events of the day, when, suddenly, we are electrified by an inhuman scream. It seems to come from outside, so the two of us rush out into the open. Another bone-splitting cry shakes us to the core. We start running towards the harbour, as we feverishly look around us to find the epicenter of the howl that seems to amplify with every step.

After some time, we can see a hole in the fence along the path, guarding the dangerous part of the island. We carefully step through, and, before long, find traces of blood everywhere. Great. I should have known. Our journalists were not going to travel back without getting to know the wildlife a little

better. Fear clutches to my heart as we follow the trail. A little further on, we find our guide lying on the ground, unconscious. We tend to him, and, after a short while, he wakes up. With a shiver in his voice, he says :
« It's the crocoboas. They took them. ».

He then explains how the actors and journalists had tried to get through the fence, and how, when attempting to stop them, he had been knocked down by one of them. Before he lost consciousness, he had heard the typical cry of the crocoboas approaching. To him, it was incomprehensible that he hadn't been eaten alive. Crocoboas are vicious creatures, and, when confronted with a fresh piece of meat, they will stop at nothing.

Levy and I look at each other. This is a real nightmare. We both know what crocoboas can do to their prey, and I have to close my eyes for a moment. It's all over. By now, our visitors are probably well inside the stomachs of our most dangerous wildlife, and, whatever is left of the press will not speak in good terms of what we have lurking about on the island. We are done for.

Levy, however, does not seem to share me in my vision of doom. He swiftly flips over to hero-mode, readies his stun gun, takes me by the arm and drags me along through the lush plantlife. He clearly thinks there's still time, and I'm not about to argue with him.

We keep following the blood patches strewn around the place, and after a while we arrive at a clearing. There's no sign of the crocoboas, but what we find instead is nothing short of blood-curdling. The clothes of the actors and journalists are strewn around, which surely means they´ve been eaten alive.

« We're too late. », Levy sinks to his knees. « They're all dead. »
I draw a deep breath, and start to see dark patches in front of my eyes.
But this time, it's my turn to play the hero.
« We have to continue, until we find them. », I manage to say. « Even if they're not alive, we have to get them back to their families. It's the only decent thing to do.»
« You won't find them. », Levy replies.
« They're well at the bottom of the lake by now. I'm afraid there is nothing we can do. »
He puts his hand on my shoulder.
« We gave it our all. But if some of the press are eaten by his animals, that's pretty much it. I really wanted this place to work out well, you know, but I'm sure this is a sign. Our project has sunk to the bottom of the lake. Let's just pray for the poor souls who've lost their lives

for us, and then get back to safety, before the crocoboas reappear. We've waited too long already. »

I hang my head in defeat. I did not think it would end like this. There were so many things we could have achieved with this island, so many things we could have taught our children, but it's all over now. The dream is crushed, and countless families will be crying tonight at the loss of their dearest. With a pang, I think of the three small children which had tagged along with the actors, and I realise that there is no way in heaven or hell that I will be able to face their mothers and fathers. Ever. The least I can do is pray for them. Tears are streaming down my face as I fold my hands, together with Levy.

But suddenly, in mid-prayer, we hear a cry. It comes from nearby. Surprised, we look at each other.
« Hello ? Is anyone there ? », Levy screams out, as we head for the direction it comes from. Feverishly, we look left and right. But we can see no-one. Suddenly, a yelp comes from above us.
« Up here ! », we hear, and, shellshocked, we gaze upwards. There they are, way up in the trees, waving and screaming for our attention.

It's a miracle. They're all there, every single one of them. No-one got eaten, no-one lost so much as a finger. Levy and I are gobsmacked. Somehow, they'd all managed to climb to safety. The children seem to be allright, except for the nasty shock they'd gotten, and Levy and I carefully help them all down from the trees.

As soon as their feet hit the ground, the actors embrace us with a giant hug. They are inordinately relieved their ordeal is over. The journalists, however, huddle up a little away from us. They seem ashamed of their acts, and dare not look us in the eye. They have endangered the lives of several people and seem extremely uncomfortable with it. But we don't have time for the blaming game. As Levy points out, we are not in safety yet. His gun at the ready, he rushes us out of the clearing, down the path, and back through the hole in the fence. We leave it to the crew to patch the hole up, and head back to the encampment. When we arrive, we serve the children a hot cacao, and the adults something stronger.

After our visitors' nerves have calmed down a bit, they tell us what had happened. The journalists had wanted to take a picture with some of our animals, and had found a way to getting through the fence. After knocking down their guide, they'd headed towards the deepest part of the jungle. It hadn't taken long before they'd been discovered by the crocoboas, and one of the actors had cast his clothes towards them in order to distract them. Unfortunately, that had only sharpened the reptiles' appetite. Shredding the clothes to pieces, they had drawn closer and closer. Our visitors were mentally preparing to be eaten alive, when a flock of flying creatures had come down from the sky. They had formed a circle around them, as if to protect them. For a minute, the crocoboas had seemed so awe-struck by the birds, that they had retracted, which had given both the journalists and the actors just enough time to climb up the trees and into safety.

When asked by Levy, the actors tried to explain what the birds looked like. We realised it had to be the peagles, half peacock, half eagle. They're the only animals the crocoboas are scared of on a permanent basis, since the peagles are much more powerful than them. Their claws can do some major damage, and their beaks are sharper than reptile skin. How the peagles had picked up on the danger our visitors were in, is a mystery, however.

When their story is finished, Levy orders some sandwiches for all of us, takes a deep breath, and then goes over to the journalists. He sits down with one of them. The man looks tired and worn. Before Levy has a chance to say anything at all, the man turns to him and says :

« Thank you for saving us. We didn't think we would get out of there alive. »

Levy shrugs, mutters a « You're welcome » and then apprehensively waits for what's bound to come next. The press will trash the « Save the planet » project and we'll all be back to square one. Paradise Island is over.

But, unbelievably, the man shakes Levy's hand and says :

« I think we have a good story now. Just wait for the paper to get out on Monday. You won't be disappointed. », and he gives him a reassuring wink before digging into the sandwiches.

Chapter Thirteen :

Back Home

I put down the newspaper, and happily gaze through the window. We've done it. The future of Paradise Island looks bright again. In the article, Mr. Browning, the journalist we talked to last weekend, has painted a fantastical picture of the wild variety of animals we have in store for the school-dwelling teen. « The Planet Saved Us», the title reads, and a vivid recollection of past events with peagles saving the lives of innocent people, is recounted. I am rather proud of myself, as I admire the picture they took of my boss, Levy and I. My hair looks amazing, and I sport a professional yet adventurous look that is bound to attract even the most hardened sceptic to the island.

School bookings have been coming in all morning, Levy told me over the phone, and as I sip from my cup of tea, I sit back in my old sofa and reminesce. The past three weeks have been magnificent, give or take a lethal attack or two, and I can't wait to visit the island again in a week from now. By then, everything should be up and running, and hoards of school children will be treasure-hunting around the picturesque surroundings immortalised by the newspaper.
Life, in other words, couldn't be better.

My boss calls me on the phone, and

tells me there is good news and bad news. My heart stops. Will he pull out of our project after all ? God knows we need the money, so, with shaky nerves, I ask him to tell me the bad news first. He plainly states that he didn't win the lottery after all, then laughs at my dumbfounded silence.

« Got you there, kiddo ! », he grins. « You didn't think I had second thoughts now, did you ? »

I feel like pulling him through the phone line and giving him a piece of my mind. But he is my boss, after all, and I politely muster a smile.

« So, what's the good news ? », I ask him, tentatively.

« Well... », he drags the moment out. « You're no longer working for me. », he states. My first reaction is utter panick, but then I realise I can hear him smile through the phone.

« What do you mean ? », I say, unsure of where this is going.

« Well, you've been headhunted, my dear. Apparently, someone thought your skills were wasted as an advertiser, and they offered you a job as head of the welcoming team on Paradise Island. »

Levy. I knew it. The little rascal. How dare he go behind my back like that ?

« You can say no, of course, », my boss

continues dryly, « but it's an awful lot of money to turn down. And come to think of it, you weren't that good an advertiser after all. I just kept you for your good looks. », he teases me. « Did you see your picture in the newspaper, by the way ? Your hair is amazing ! », he chuckles. « I'll be sorry to see you leave. »

I grin. « Finally some respect for my hairdo. », I say, playing along. « I knew those five hours in the bathroom would pay off. » We both laugh.
« So, that's it, then. », he continues. « You're off to your next adventure. Any famous last words, before we part ? »
« Yes. », I say, without further ado. « Will you come and visit us now and again ? You and your little chequebook are our heroes, you know. We can't live without you.», I tease him.
« Are you kidding me ? Of course I will ! I can't wait to be eaten alive by whatever you breed next on that island ! », he grins. « And I'm dying to eat more of that omelet you serve. I still haven't figured out what that funny little taste is. »
« It's one of our kitchen secrets. », I say sternly. « You'd have to bribe me to tell you what it is. »
« You don't know, do you ? », he says playfully.

« I do, but if I tell you, you´d never touch the stuff again. »

He laughs.

« So, any news of the crocoboas ? », he continues. « What are you going to do with them ? »

« We'll have to put them down. », I sigh miserably. « No zoo in their right mind wants them, and, even if we keep them locked up behind fences, there is always the threat of them breaking out. Or of curious children of breaking in. We simply cannot afford to keep them alive. It's too dangerous. Poor things.»

« Don't tell me you're going all soft on those so-called harmless, flesh-eating creatures. You nearly lost ten people over there. »

« I know. But still, it's tough to have to end their lives, even if they are nasty reptiles. We created them, you know, so it's a bit like killing your own children. »

« Wow. Okay, I didn't see that one coming. Motherly feelings for a bunch of vicious man-eating-creatures. Maybe I didn't give you enough credit. You would have made a brilliant head of the advertising team, after all. », he chuckles.

« Well, it's a bit late for that now, isn't it ? », I say. « You just gave me away to the highest bidder. You'll miss me dearly, I'm telling you. »

« I know. », he sighs. « Life will be a bit more

boring around the office now. But hey, I'm sure you'll make the best of it on Paradise Island. They need people there who can tame a flyon or two, and God knows you've tamed me and my chequebook into submission. »

« A flyon ? », I ask, perplexed.

« Well, if you have flygers, you should have flyons, too, don't you think ? »

« I laugh. « Good idea. Maybe I'll give you a job, as head of our creative team. »

« Me, work for you ? In what world ? Plus, I'd like to keep all my limbs for the moment, thank you very much. But I appreciate your asking, I'm really flattered. »

We laugh and our phone conversation draws to an end. I go and sit down on the sofa again, when suddenly, the doorbell rings. It's Suze. She's standing in the doorway, all lit up like a Christmas tree.

« I read the paper ! », she beams. « Well, aren't you the talk of the day, missie ? The whole town is buzzing ! I've never been so busy in my life, having people over for tea and telling them all your adventures. »

« But I haven't spoken to you since I've been back. », I object.

« I know ! », she smiles up to her ears. « All the more fun for me ! »

I look at her in desperation. The woman is unstoppable. Heaven knows what's she's been telling innocent bystanders.

« Speaking of fun... », she says, with a mysterious smile. « I have brought a guest with me. »

She steps aside, and I find myself face to face with Special Agent Forrester.

« I just thought I'd ask him round, so you could tell him all about your adventures. », she rattles on. « And I'm sure he'll be more than happy to accompany you on your next trip, won't you, Special Agent Forrester ? » she flirts. Then, closer to my ear: « Be nice. I won't keep doing you favours like this, you know.» And, with a wink, she disappears.

Embarrassed, I ask him to sit down with me and pour him a cup of tea. The poor man seems just as rattled I am, so I take pity on him and open the conversation.

« So, Suze,... », I say, tentatively.

« Yes... », he sighs.

« Some character, huh ? », I continue.

« Indeed. », he says, and shifts around nervously. He's clearly uncomfortable with my line of questioning, and looks unsure as to what my relationship to her is. Are we good friends, or mortal ennemies ? He decides to play it safe, and says nothing at all.

Then, after a little while :

« I've seen your picture in the newspaper. »

« Yes ? »

« It was nice. I liked your hair. I mean... », and he trails off, blushing to the bone.

I raise my eyebrows in surprise. Really ? A compliment ? From him ? I sit and secretly wonder what on earth Suze has told him about me.

« I mean... », he continues. «... I'm sorry that I sort of threatened you the other night... »

« Sort of ? « , I reply, a little louder than I intended. « You scared the bejeezes out of me ! »

« I hope you can forgive me. », he looks at the floor . « It's my job, you see. It's what I do. I get paid for it. »

« Lucky you. », I reply sarcastically. « You must have a lot of friends. »

He gives me a forlorn look.

« So I thought... », he continues.

« Yes ? »

« Well, I figured that maybe... ? »

Oh come on, man, spit it out, I think.

He seems to be mustering all the courage he has. « Would...would you like to have dinner with me some time? » His blush deepens to crimson, and I realise I have to say something before he turns all blue.

« Sure. », I reply. « On one condition. »

«Okay...what condition? », he shoots me a nervous look.

« As long as it´s not at The Black Swan. It´s incredible, the types you meet there.» I say and flash him my most playful smile.

He laughs. « Good, that's settled then. I'll pick you up at seven. », he says and gets up.

« Right. », I say. « Just one more thing . »

« Yes ? »

« I don't believe I know your first name. »

« It's Reginald. », he says, pleasantly.

« Pleased to meet you, Reginald. I'm Melissa. », and I shake his hand.

« I know. », he says dryly. « You're in my files. »

This time, it's my turn to blush.

« So, what else is in those files of yours ? », I say, twisting my hair rather playfully.

Alas, my inexperienced flirting attempt hits rock-bottom, as he says : « It's best you don't know. I don't want you to lie awake at night. » And he leaves me standing by the door.

I sigh and sit down again. Once more, it's been proven. Flirting does not work for me. And heaven only knows what's in those files. But hey, there's good news too. I have a new, much more exciting job now. I wonder what it will be like, working on Paradise Island. I'm rather looking forward to it, and gladly think of all the animals I'll befriend over the next few months.

Suddenly, I remember Furball. I really have to give Levy a call and ask about him. Has he changed back into a rabbit yet ? Levy seems to think he will alternate between being a phoenix and a critter for all times, and we all have a bet going on as to when that will be next. I kind of miss him, now that I'm back in my empty apartment. I give his cage a melancholy look, and take a peek at the clock. I still have a few hours to kill before Reginald picks me up. So I decide, right there and then, it is time for action. Time to pay a Furball's friends a visit. But instead of heading off to Paradise Island, I decide to put on my jacket, open the door, and, with a big smile on my face, head for the pet shop around the corner

© 2025 Katleen Nielsen
Publisher: BoD · Books on Demand,
Strandvejen 100, 2900 Hellerup, bod@bod.dk
Print: Libri Plureos GmbH, Friedensallee 273,
22763 Hamborg, Tyskland
ISBN: 978-8-7717-0243-9

FSC
www.fsc.org

MIX

Papir fra
ansvarlige kilder
Paper from
responsible sources

FSC® C105338